This Book Belongs To:

Johnny Euan Buchan.

with love

Granda & Grandma
Christmas
2005

Mick Inkpen's
Kipper
and Friends

Mick Inkpen's
Kipper
and Friends

h

*Hodder
Children's
Books*

A division of Hodder Headline Limited

Contents

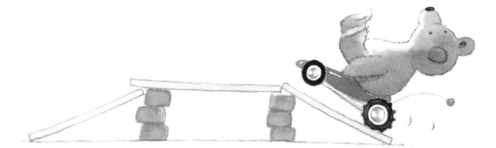

Kipper

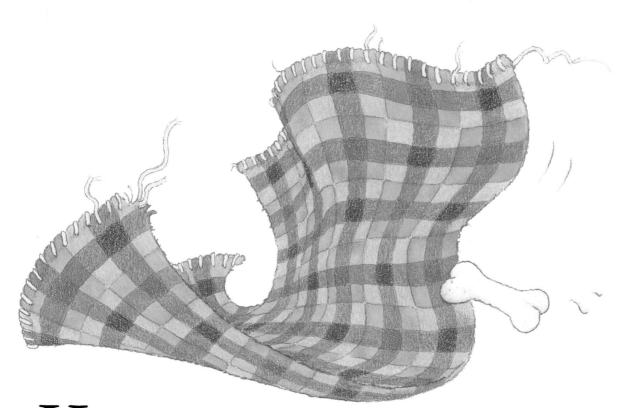

Kipper was in the mood for tidying his basket.

'You are falling apart!' he said to his rabbit.

'You are chewed and you are soggy!' he said to his ball and his bone.

'And you are DISGUSTING!' he said to his smelly old blanket.

Out they went.
'That's better!' said Kipper.

Ⓑut it was not better. Now his
basket was uncomfortable.

He twisted and he turned.
He wiggled and he wriggled.
But it was no good. He could
not get comfortable.

'Silly basket!' said Kipper…

…and went outside.

Outside there were two ducks.
They looked very comfortable
standing on one leg.

'That's what I should do!' said
Kipper. But he wasn't very good.
He could only…

...wobble.

Some wrens had made a nest inside a flowerpot. It looked very cosy.

'I should sleep in one of those!' said Kipper. But Kipper would not fit inside a flowerpot.

He was much too big!

The squirrels had made their nest
out of sticks.

'I will build myself a stick nest!'
said Kipper. But Kipper's nest was
not very good. He could only find...

...three sticks!

The sheep looked very happy
just sitting in the grass.
No, that was no good either.
The grass was much too...

...tickly!

The frog had found a sunny place
in the middle of the pond.
He was sitting on a lily pad.
'I wonder if I could do that,'
said Kipper.

But he couldn't!

'Perhaps a nice dark hole
would be good,' thought Kipper.
'The rabbits seem to like them.'

But it was not
a rabbit hole!

Kipper rushed indoors and hid underneath his blanket.

His

lovely

old

smelly

blanket!

Kipper put the blanket back in
his basket. He found his rabbit.
'Sorry Rabbit,' he said.
He found his bone and his ball.
'I like my basket just the way it is,'
yawned Kipper. He climbed in and
pulled the blanket over his head.
'It is the best basket in
the whole, wide…

. . . sssssssssssshh

hhhhhhh!

One Bear
at Bedtime

1

One bear at bedtime
is all I need...

2

I have two pigs
who wear my clothes…

3

Three kangaroos
who bounce on my bed…

4

Four giraffes
who sit in the bath…

5

Five lions who
mess about with
the shampoo…

6

Six snakes who
unwind the toilet roll…

7

Seven ostriches
who drink my milk…

8

Eight crocodiles
who use up all the
toothpaste…

9

Nine caterpillars
who crawl about at night…
(Did you spot them?)

10

And a monster
with ten heads
who takes forever
to say goodnight.

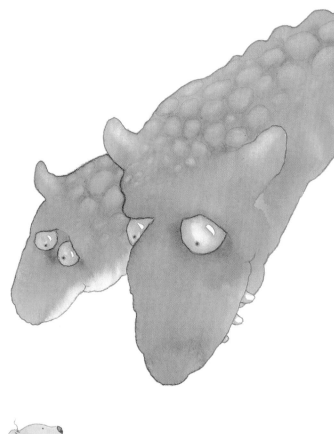

But one bear at bedtime…

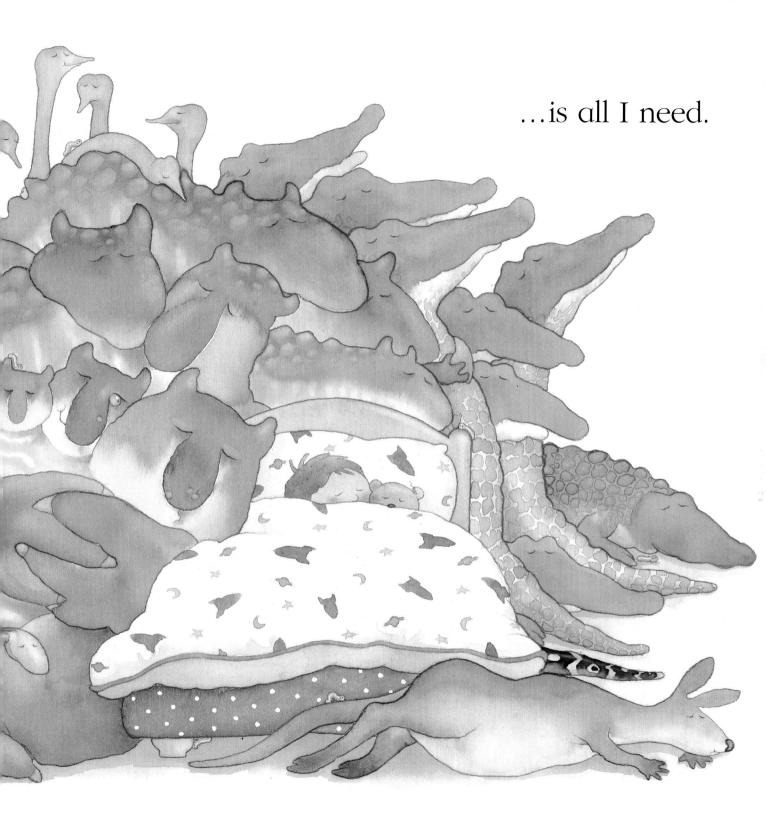

...is all I need.

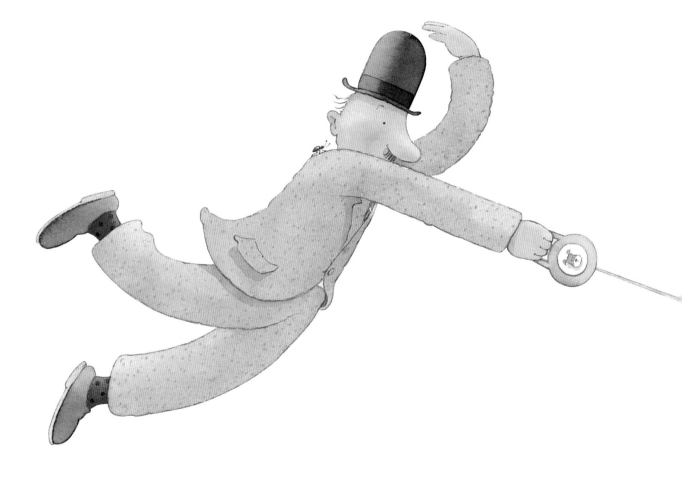

Billy's Beetle

Billy had a beetle in a matchbox.
Or rather he hadn't. He had lost it.
Silly Billy.

'Have you seen my beetle?' he asked
the girl. But she hadn't.

Along came a man with a sniffy dog.
'Don't you worry!' said the man with
the sniffy dog. 'My sniffy dog will soon
find your beetle!'
Off went the sniffy dog.
Sniff.Sniff.Sniff.

Soon the sniffy dog had found a hedgehog, two spiders, some worms and a bone.
But not the beetle.

'I will help find Billy's beetle,' said the hedgehog. And so the search continued.

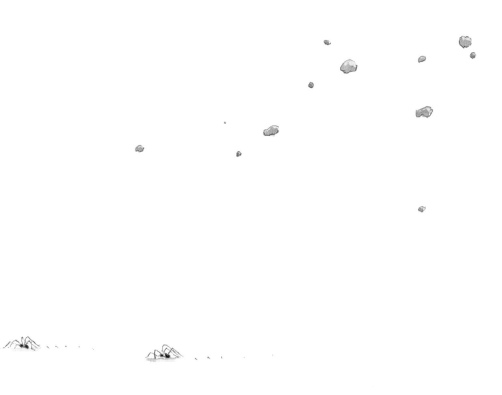

Suddenly, the sniffy dog stopped digging
and took off like a rocket!
'Look at him go!' said the man.
'He can smell Billy's beetle!'

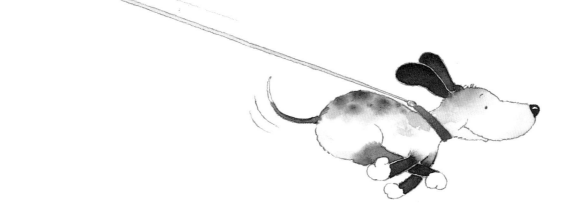

But the sniffy dog had not smelled Billy's beetle.
He had smelled sausages.

'Leave, sniffy dog! Leave!' said the man.
So the sniffy dog grabbed the sausages,
and left!

Now there was Billy, the girl, the hedgehog,
the sniffy dog, the man with the sniffy dog,
and the woman without the sausages,
all looking for Billy's beetle.
(And a polar bear who had joined in for fun.)

The sniffy dog found a tuba. It belonged to a man in an oompah band.

'I don't think Billy's beetle is in there,' said the bandsman. 'But we will help you look.'

So the oompah band played and off they went again. Oompah! Oompah! Sniff, sniff, sniff!

An elephant wandered over to see what all
the fuss was about.

'Stand aside!' said the man with the sniffy dog.
'My sniffy dog is looking for this boy's beetle!'
The elephant became very excited.

'I've seen it!' he said.

The elephant jumped up and down and pointed
with his trunk.

'Is THAT the beetle?' he trumpeted triumphantly.

'No,' said Billy. 'That is not my beetle.
That is a furry caterpillar.'

Instantly the elephant was untriumphant and untrumpetible. He sat down.

The girl sighed a long, long sigh and sat down too.

'Where can it be?' she said.

The man with the sniffy dog, the sniffy dog, the lady without the sausages, the polar bear and the oompah band sat down next to them.

But the hedgehog was hopping from one foot to the other, and pointing.

'The beetle! It's the beetle!' he squeaked.

'We've found the beetle! We've found the beetle!'
'HOORAY! HOORAY! HOORAY!' they shouted.

'BUT WHERE IS BILLY?' said the girl.
Everybody stopped shouting. They looked up.
They looked down. They looked behind, in front,
and in between. But Billy had disappeared.

'Don't you worry!' said the man with the
sniffy dog. 'My sniffy dog has found something!'

'BUT WHERE IS BILLY?' said the girl.
Everybody stopped shouting. They looked up.
They looked down. They looked behind, in front,
and in between. But Billy had disappeared.

'Don't you worry!' said the man with the
sniffy dog. 'My sniffy dog has found something!'

But the sniffy dog had not found Billy.
He had found a little pig.
    'Excuse me,' said the little pig.
'I have lost my furry caterpillar.
Have you seen him?'

So the girl, the sniffy dog, the man with the
sniffy dog, the hedgehog, the woman without the
sausages, the polar bear, the oompah band,
the elephant, the little pig AND the beetle
all went off together to look for Billy
and the furry caterpillar.

And once again
it was the hedgehog
who found them...

...and the sniffy dog who didn't!

The
Blue
Balloon

The day after my birthday party
Kipper found a soggy blue balloon
in the garden.

It was odd because the balloons
at my party were red and white.

I blew it up.

At first I thought it was
just an ordinary balloon.
But now I am not so sure.

It is shiny and squeaky and
you can make rude noises with it.
    And if you give it a rub you can
stick it on the ceiling.
    Just like an ordinary balloon.

But there is something odd about my balloon.

It doesn't matter how much you blow it up, it just goes on getting bigger . . .

You see it never ever bursts. Never ever.

I have squeezed it . . .   squashed it . . .

. . . and whacked it with a stick.

I have kicked it . . .   run it over . . .

. . . and stretched it!

And Kipper has attacked it.
But it is Indestructible.

I think that my balloon has
Strange and Wonderful Powers!

The other day it disappeared completely . . .

. . . and when it came back it was square!

And this morning, while I was taking it for a walk . . .

and up . . .   Oops!

It took me up . . .   and up . . .

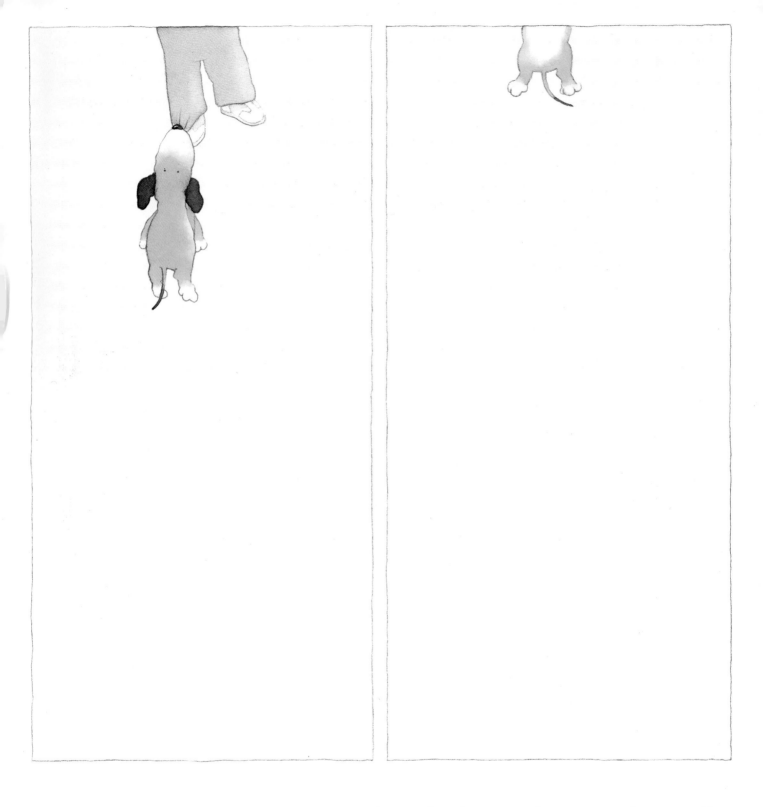

. . . it decided to take me for a fly!

And finally . . .   . . . down.

It was quite a trip, but we were back in time for tea.

So if you find a soggy old balloon . . .

. . . whatever you do
don't throw it away.

Especially if it's a blue one.

You never know what it will do next.

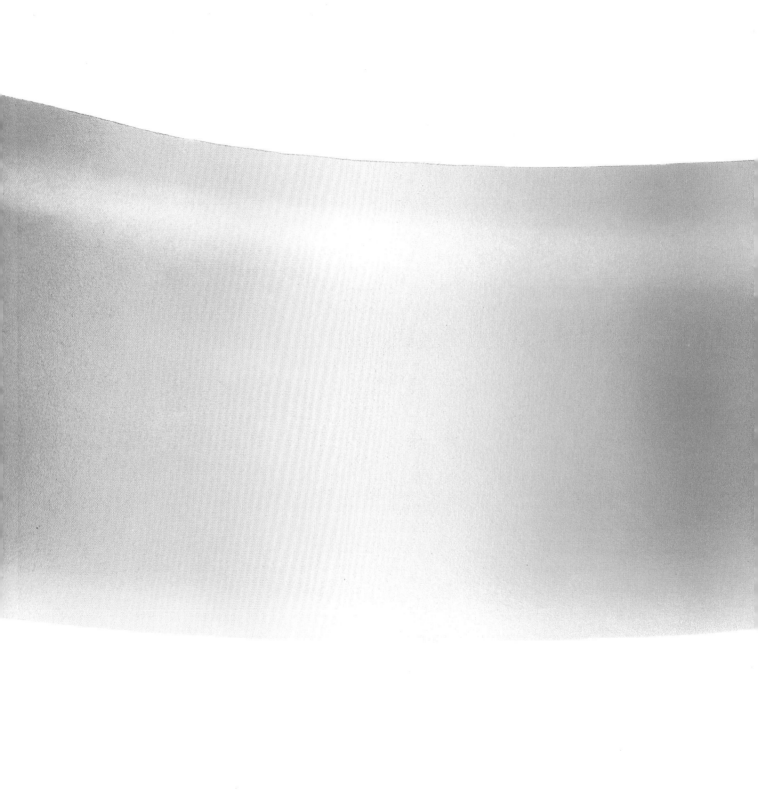

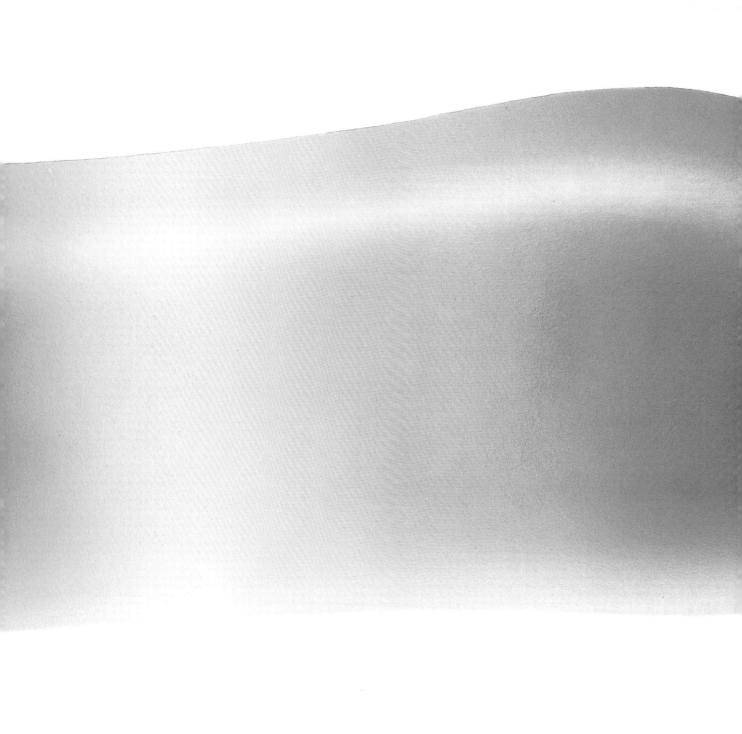

Threadbear

 Ben's bear was called
Threadbear. He was old.
Bits of him had worn
out. Or worked loose.
Or dropped off.

He had a paw which
didn't match, and a button
for an eye. When he looked
through the button he saw four pictures
instead of one. It was like looking in a
television shop window.

But there was one thing that had always
been wrong with Threadbear. The silly man who
had made him had put too much stuffing inside
him. His arms were too hard. His legs were too
hard. And there was so much stuffing inside his
tummy that his squeaker had been squashed.
It had never squeaked. Not even once.

Threadbear hated having a squeaker in his tummy that wouldn't squeak. It made him feel that he was letting Ben down.

Ben's frog could croak. His space monster could squelch. And his electronic robot could burble away for hours if its batteries were the right way round.

Even the little toy that Ben called Grey Thing could make a noise, and nobody knew what Grey Thing was meant to be!

Nobody could make Threadbear's squeaker work.

Ben's dad couldn't do it.   His mum couldn't do it.

Nor could his auntie or his grandma.

Nor could any
of his friends.

When Ben had measles he asked the doctor about Threadbear's squeaker.

The doctor listened to Threadbear's tummy. But there was no squeak. Not even the faintest sign of one.

The other toys tried to help.

'If you had a winder like me, we could wind you up,' said Frog.

'If you were made of rubber like me, we could squelch you,' said the space monster.

'If you had batteries like me, we could turn you on,' said the robot. It was not much help.

'Why don't you ask Father Christmas?' said Grey Thing. 'He knows all about toys.'

This was a brilliant idea and Grey Thing went a little pink.

'But where does Father Christmas live?' asked Threadbear.

'At a place called the North Pole,' said Grey Thing. 'You can get to it up the chimney I think.'

Threadbear had never climbed up a chimney before. It was hard work. He took a wrong turn and fell back down. But he did not give up.

It was long after bedtime when Threadbear poked his head out of the chimney pot.

This must be the North Pole!

Threadbear sat down to wait for Father Christmas. He waited and waited. But Father Christmas did not seem to be coming.

The moon rose into the sky and Threadbear began to doze . . .

They flew over the top of the world and on to the land where the squeaker trees grow.

It tasted delicious but it made
Threadbear feel sleepy.

Threadbear felt himself
falling and falling...

Suddenly Father Christmas was there
helping Threadbear into his sleigh!

'You must eat the biggest squeaker fruit,'
said Father Christmas.

Threadbear could hear the squeaker
trees as they came in to land.

Bump! Threadbear woke up. He rubbed his eyes and looked around. There was no squeaker fruit, no squeaker tree and worst of all no Father Christmas.

'I must have fallen asleep and dropped off the North Pole!' said Threadbear.

In the morning Ben was surprised to find Threadbear in the garden covered with soot. Ben's mum put Threadbear straight into the washing machine. She did not even look at the label on Threadbear's neck which read in capital letters DO NOT WASH!

When Threadbear came out of the washing machine the soot was gone, but there was a curious purple stain on his chin, which nobody could explain. Threadbear was feeling too giddy to notice. His head felt like a spinning top!

'I don't mind feeling giddy,' thought
Threadbear as he hung on the line.
'I don't mind having a button for an
eye and a paw that doesn't match.
I don't even mind being hung up by the
ear. But what I DO mind, what I mind
VERY MUCH is having a silly
squeaker in my tummy
that won't SQUEAK!'

Threadbear was so cross that he
frightened a robin. It flew away leaving
him alone in the garden bouncing angry
little bounces on the washing line.

The sun rose slowly over the garden.
It shone straight down on Threadbear,
a great warm shine like an enormous hug.
Threadbear began to steam. He began to
feel better. The more he steamed the
better he felt.

He swung his legs backwards and
forwards. Then he kicked them high in the
air. Soon he was swinging round and round
the washing line giggling to himself.

'Why do I feel so happy?' he wondered.

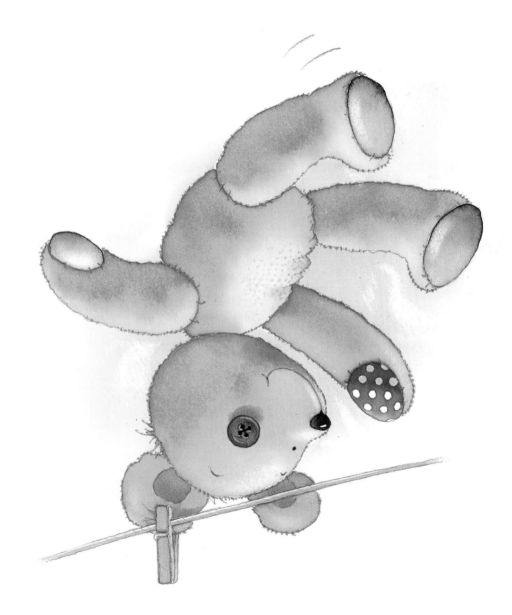

It was at this moment that Threadbear realised a very odd thing had happened to him. His paws felt different. So did his arms and his legs. They were no longer hard!

And inside his tummy was a wonderful, loose, comfortable feeling that he had never felt before!

At the very same moment something caught Threadbear's eye. Something red was racing across the sun. And to Threadbear's surprise the red something was waving goodbye!

W hen Ben came out to see
if Threadbear was dry he
noticed that his little brown
bear had changed.
'Look mum,' said Ben,
'He's gone floppy!'
Ben's mum unpegged
Threadbear's ear. 'Oh dear!' she said,
'His stuffing must have shrunk in the wash!'
Ben looked at Threadbear. 'I like him
like that. It makes him look...' But Ben
could not think of the right word so instead
he gave Threadbear a squeeze.
And for the first time the squeaker
in Threadbear's tummy gave the
loudest,
clearest,
squeakiest...

. . . squeak!

Lullabyhullaballoo!

The sun is down.
The moon is up.
It is bedtime for the
Little Princess.
But outside the castle…

A dragon is roaring.
What shall we do?
He's hissing and snorting!
What shall we do?
We'll tell him to SSSH!
That's what we'll do.

SSSH!

But,

The brave knights are clanking.

What shall we do?

They're rattling and clunking!

What shall we do?

We'll tell them to SSSH!

That's what we'll do.

SSSH!

But,

The brave knights are clanking.
What shall we do?
They're rattling and clunking!
What shall we do?
We'll tell them to SSSH!
That's what we'll do.

SSSH!

YES YOU!

But,

The ghosts are oooooing.
What shall we do?
They're ooo ooo oooooing!
What shall we do?
We'll tell them to SSSH!
That's what we'll do.

SSSH!

But,

Out in the forest

Wolves are howling

Owls are hooting

Frogs are croaking

Mice are squeaking

Bats are flapping

Bears are growling

Y_{ES DO}!

B ut,

The giant is stamping.
What shall we do?
He's galumphing and stomping!
What shall we do?
We'll tell him to SSSH!
That's what we'll do.

SSSH!

Yes yooooooooo!

YES YOU!

B ut,

The ghosts are oooooing.
What shall we do?
They're ooo ooo oooooing!
What shall we do?
We'll tell them to SSSH!
That's what we'll do.

SSSH!

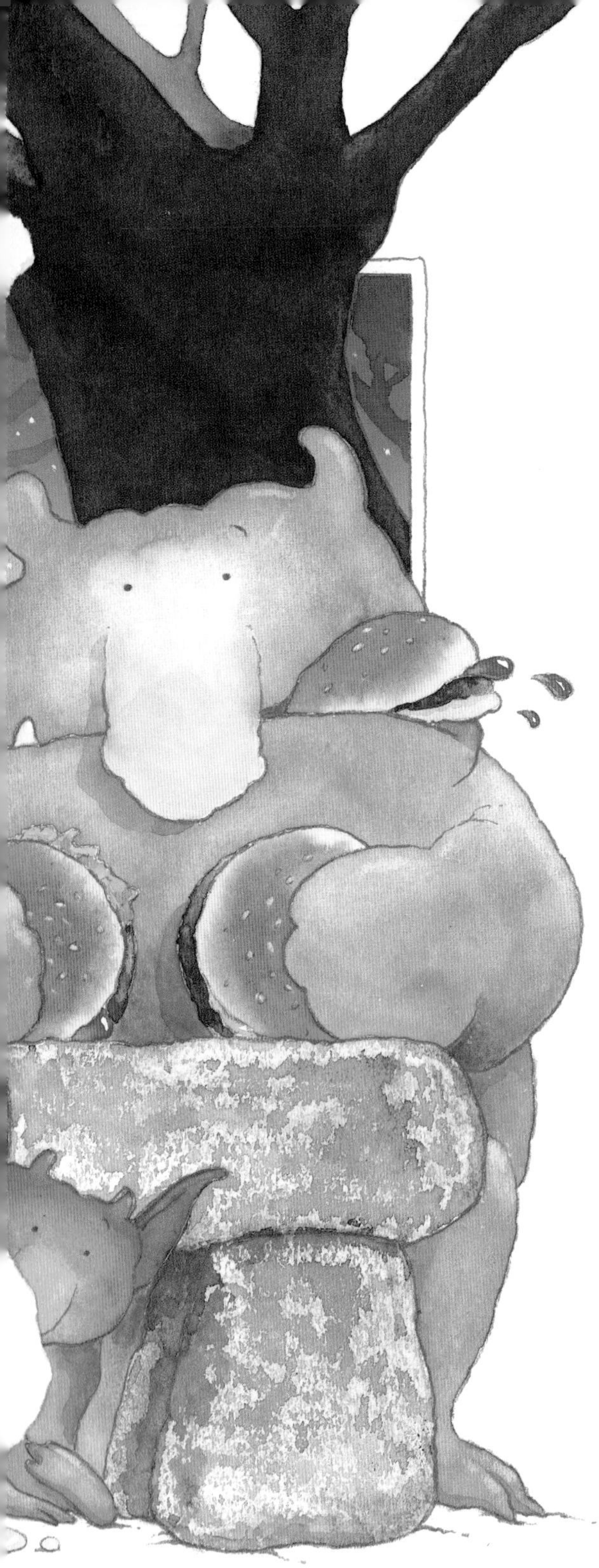

And the trolls
and the goblins
are guzzling
and gobbling
and slurping
and burping!

What shall we do?

We'll tell them to…

...STOP!

Βut now,
The Princess is crying!
What shall we do?
She won't stop howling!
What shall we do?
We'll sing her a lullaby.
That's what we'll do.
We'll ALL sing a lullaby.

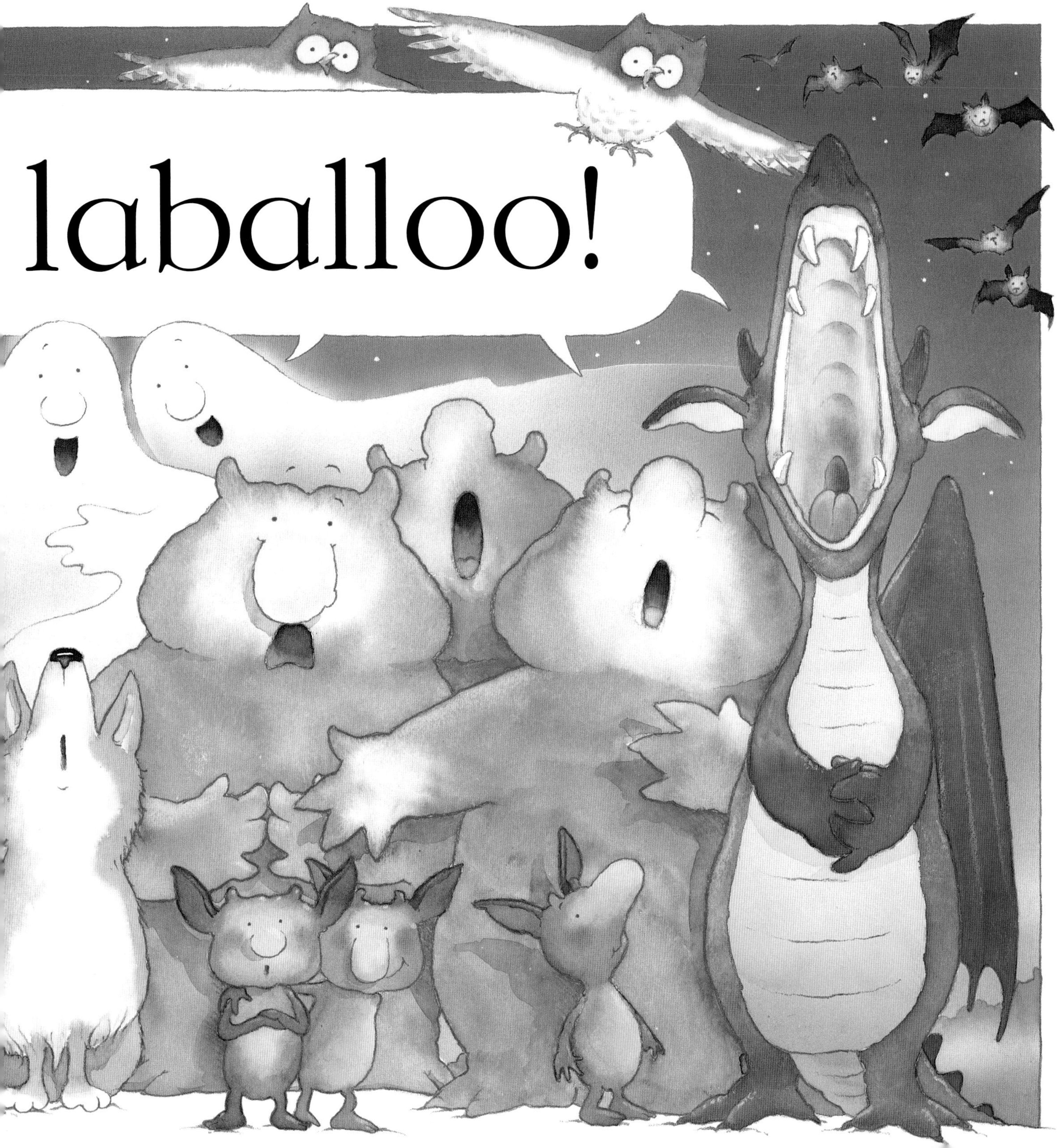
laballoo!

Now the Princess is smiling.

Her eyelids are drooping.

The Princess is sleeping.

So what shall we do?
We'll tiptoe to bed
And we shall sleep too.
We shall sleep too.

But,

S
snore!

snore!

But,

snore!

snore!

nore!

snore!

snore!

snore!

snore!

….the Princess is snoring!
What *shall* we do?

Bear

A small whooshing sound.
Then a plop!
A bounce.
And a kind of squeak.
That was how the bear landed
in my baby sister's playpen.

Have you ever had a bear fall out of the sky, right in front of you? At first I thought he was a teddy bear. He just lay there, crumpled on the quilt.

Then he got up and took Sophie's drink. And her biscuit. That's when I knew he was real.

The bear climbed out of the playpen
and looked at me.

He rolled on his back, lifted his
paws and growled.
He seemed to
want to play.

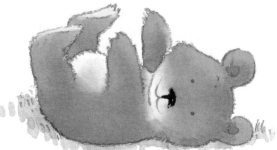

I put him in
Sophie's baby bouncer.
He was very good at bouncing,
much better than Sophie.

I sneaked the bear into the house under the quilt. At bedtime I hid him among my toys.

'Don't you say anything, Sophie!' I said. 'I want to keep this bear.'

Sophie doesn't say much anyway. She isn't even two yet.

In the morning the sound of shouting woke me up.

'Sophie, that's naughty!' It was Mum.
She was looking at the feathers.

'Sophie! That's very naughty!'
She was looking at the scribble.

Then she looked at the potty.

'Sophie!' she said. 'Good girl!'

But I don't think it
was Sophie.

I'm sure it wasn't Sophie.

It definitely wasn't
Sophie.

I took the bear to
school in my rucksack.
Everyone wanted to be
my friend.
'Does he bite?' they said.
'He doesn't bite me,'
I said.
'What's his name?'
they said.
'He doesn't
have one.'

We kept him quiet all day
feeding him our lunches. He liked
the peanut butter sandwiches best.

After school my friends came to the house.

'Where is he?' they said.

We played with the bear behind the garage.

We made a
tunnel…

a bridge…

and a jump!

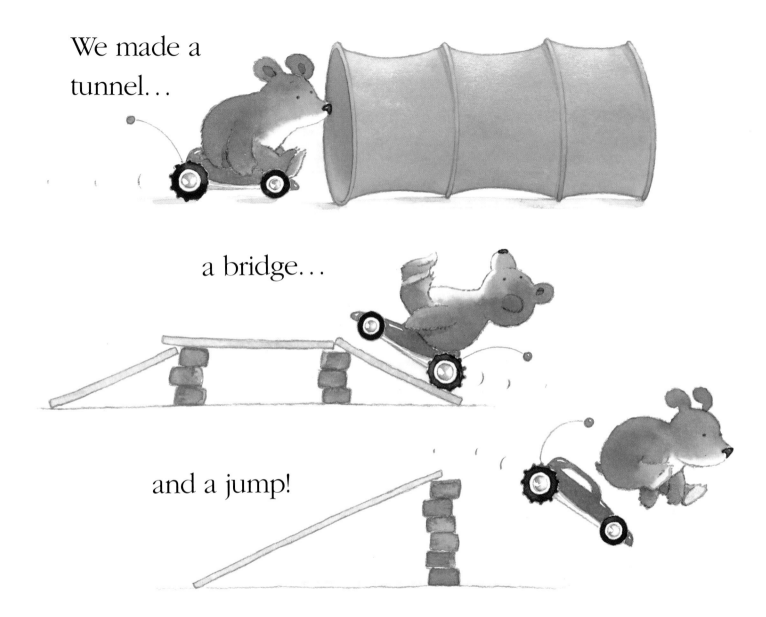

When the car came back the bear
had gone. We looked and looked
but there was no bear anywhere.

At bedtime Sophie
wouldn't go to sleep.
　　She didn't want her elephant.
She didn't want her rabbit.
She threw them out of the cot.
　　I gave her my second best pig.
She threw it out.
　　'Sophie! That's naughty!'
said Mum.
　　But Sophie just howled.
She wanted the bear.

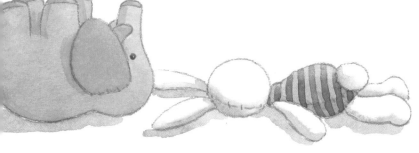

CRASH! BANG!
It was the middle
of the night.
SMASH! CLANG!
The noise was coming from
the kitchen. We crept downstairs
and peeped through the door.
It wasn't a burglar.

'Bear!' said Sophie. 'Naughty!'

So today a serious man in a serious hat came to look at our bear. He wrote something in a big black book.

'Will you have to take him away?' I said.

'We nearly always do,' said the man. He pointed his pen at my bear. 'But,' he said, 'this bear is an Exception.'

'This bear,' he went on, 'has fallen quite unexpectedly into a storybook. And it is not up to me to say what should happen next.'

'So can we keep him?' I said.

'Ask them,' he said. And he
pointed straight out of the picture
at YOU!

And you thought for a moment.
You looked at the man.
You looked at the bear.
You looked at Sophie.
You looked at me.

And then you said...

'YES YOU CAN!'

So we did.

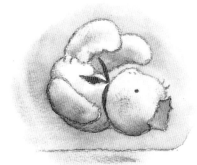

Nothing

A new baby is on the way.
The family are moving out of Number
47 to a bigger house round the corner.
The cat has gone missing. But
everything else is packed and ready
to go.

Nothing has been left behind...

The little thing in the attic at
Number 47 had forgotten all about
daylight. It had been squashed in the
dark for so long that it could remember
very little of anything. Stuck beneath
years of junk, it could not recall how it
felt to stand up, or to stretch out its arms.
So long had it been there, even its own
name was lost.

'I wonder who I am,'
it thought. But it
could not remember.

The day came when the family that lived at Number 47 were to move.

All day long the little thing listened to thuds and thumps and the sound of tramping feet in the house below, until at last the attic door was flung open and large hands began to stuff cardboard boxes full of junk.

The little thing felt the weight on top of it gradually lighten, and suddenly the glare of a torch beam stung its eyes.

'What have we got here?' said a voice.

'Oh, it's nothing,' said another. 'Let the new people get rid of it.'

The torch was switched off. The boxes were carried out. And moments later, somewhere down below, the front door slammed shut. Number 47 was empty.

'So that's my name,' thought the little thing. 'Nothing!'

For the first time in a very long time, Nothing sat up. He looked around him at the cobwebs and shafts of dusty moonlight. Then, in the quiet, he heard the patter of feet and a mouse came running towards him.

'New People always try to get rid of you,' it said, without introducing itself. It looked at him. 'Seen you under the rug. What are you?'

'Nothing,' replied Nothing.

'Well, nothing or not, you can't stay here, not with New People coming,' said the mouse. It hurried off.

Nothing struggled to his feet. On unsteady legs he followed the dusty paw prints. The mouse stopped by a moonlit gap under the eaves.

'Through there,' it said. 'Good luck!'

With a wriggle of its tail it disappeared under the floorboards.

'I used to have a tail!' thought Nothing suddenly.
He felt sure of it.

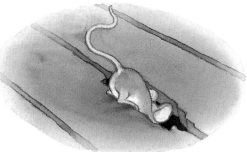

How do you think you would feel if you had been squashed in the dark for years and years. And then you squeezed through a tiny hole to find yourself under the big, starry sky?

Well, there are no words for that kind of feeling, so I won't try to tell you how Nothing felt, except to say that he sat on the roof staring up at the moon and stars for a very long time.

He was still staring upwards as he made his way along the gutter, which is why he fell straight down the drainpipe!

othing rolled into the garden and sat up.

'What on earth are you?' said a silky voice. The fox, for that is what it was, left the dustbin and trotted towards him.

'I'm Nothing,' said Nothing.

The fox sniffed at him. Its whiskers quivered. Its ears pricked.

'I used to have ears and whiskers!' thought Nothing suddenly. He was sure of it.

The fox spoke again. 'Nothing,' it said disdainfully. 'Nothing worth eating, that's for sure.' It trotted away silently.

Nothing wandered into the garden and came across a lily pond. There a frog sat gently croaking. As Nothing approached it plopped into the water and, with a kick of its stripy legs, it disappeared from view.

'I used to have stripes!' thought Nothing. 'I'm sure I did!'

The ripples cleared and Nothing found himself staring at his own reflection. It was odd. It was ugly.

'What are you?' it said to Nothing sadly. A tear rolled up its face and splashed onto the surface of the pond. The ugly face disappeared among the ripples.

'What are you?' repeated Nothing.

'I'm a cat!' said a loud voice. 'Who's asking?' A big, lolloping tabby cat tumbled out from behind a bush, and grinned at Nothing.

Nothing opened his mouth to explain that he had been talking to himself, and that he did not know what he was, and that he was lost, and that he had just been sniffed by a horrible fox, and that he was feeling very miserable. But instead he found himself shuddering and shaking, as great uncontrollable sobs quivered up his little, raggedy body and sat him on the ground.

'I don't know who I am!' he howled. 'I don't know who I am!'

The cat licked him full in the face.

After a while
Nothing stopped crying.
The cat lay down
beside him. Between
Nothing's loud sniffs it told him all about
itself. How its name was Toby. And how it
came from a long line of Tobys.

'I live in the house,' it said. 'At least I
used to. We moved round the corner
today. They think I'm lost. But it's all the
same to me. Number 47, Number 97,
what's the difference? It's all my patch.
D'you want to see?'

Nothing sniffed once more and
nodded.

'Course you do!' said the cat.
It picked up Nothing and sprang
onto the garden wall.

Nothing had never ridden
through the night in a cat's mouth before.
It whisked him up through the branches of a
tree and out onto the rooftops, where they
sped along, with the moon racing them
behind the chimney pots.

'I'm taking you the long way round,'
panted the cat. 'It's more fun!'

All the while, joggling along inside Nothing's
head, there was a thought trying to get out. It
felt like an important thought. It had something
to do with the cat.

The cat jumped the fence at Number 97 and trotted in through the back door. He found an old man dozing in a chair surrounded by unpacked boxes.

'That's Grandpa,' whispered the cat to Nothing, and dropped him on the old man's lap.

'So there you are!' said Grandpa waking up. 'What have you brought me this time?' He put on his glasses and looked at Nothing. 'Good heavens! Look everyone! Look what Toby's found!'

Nothing looked up at Grandpa and saw a face he knew. The important thought inside his head popped open like a jack-in-a-box.

The family gathered round to look.

'What is it, Grandpa?' said the children. But Grandpa was busy rummaging among the cardboard boxes.

'I know it's here somewhere,' he said. 'Ah, there it is!'

He pulled out an old photograph album and opened it, turning the pages until he came to a fading photograph of a baby.

'That's me!' he said. 'And that's Toby's Great Great Great Great Grandfather. And this,' he said, tapping the photograph and tickling Nothing's tummy with his forefinger, 'this is Little Toby!'

At last Nothing remembered who he was. Though he had no ears, nor whiskers, no tail and no stripes, he was for certain a little cloth tabby cat whose name was not Nothing, but Little Toby.

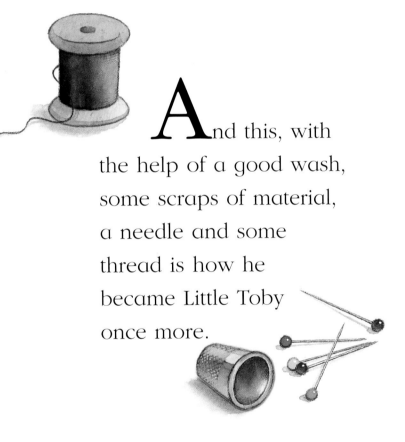

And this, with
the help of a good wash,
some scraps of material,
a needle and some
thread is how he
became Little Toby
once more.

When the new baby arrived, Little Toby
was handed back to Grandpa who tucked him
carefully in the cot.

And, straight away, the new baby began to
chew on his ear, which if it had been your ear would
probably have hurt a little, but since it belonged
to a little cloth cat, did not hurt in the slightest.

When the new baby arrived, Little Toby
was handed back to Grandpa who tucked him
carefully in the cot.

   And, straight away, the new baby began to
chew on his ear, which if it had been your ear would
probably have hurt a little, but since it belonged
to a little cloth cat, did not hurt in the slightest.

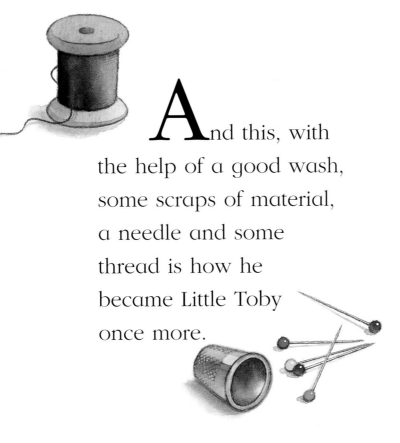

And this, with the help of a good wash, some scraps of material, a needle and some thread is how he became Little Toby once more.

Kipper's Birthday

It was the day before Kipper's birthday. He was busy with his paints making party invitations. In large letters he painted,

Plees come to my bithday party tomoro at 12 o cloc dont be lat

He hung them up to dry and set about making a cake.

Kipper had not made a cake before. He put some currants and eggs and currants and flour and sugar and currants into a bowl. Then he stirred the mixture until his arm ached.

Next he added some cherries and stirred it once more. Then he rolled it with a rolling pin and looked at what he had made.

'I have made a flat thing,' he said.

Kipper squeezed the flat thing into
a cake shape and watched it bake in the
oven. To his surprise it changed itself
slowly into a sort of heap, but it
smelled good. He put the last remaining
cherry on the top for decoration.

By this time the party invitations
were dry.

'I'll deliver them tomorrow,' yawned
Kipper. 'It's too late now.'

Kipper woke bright and early on his birthday. His first thought was, 'Balloons! We must have balloons!' But as he rushed downstairs another thought popped into his head. 'Invitations!'

Kipper ran all the way to his best friend's house and stuffed the invitations into Tiger's hand.

'That one's yours! Those are for the others!' he panted. 'Can't stop! Balloons!'

When he had gone Tiger opened the invitation.

Plees come to my bithday party tomoro at 12 o cloc dont be lat

At twelve o'clock Kipper carefully placed his cake on the table and sat down to wait for a knock at the door.

He waited. And he waited. But nobody came. Not even Tiger.

The cake smelled good and Kipper began to feel hungry. At one o'clock he ate the cherry from the top.

Two o'clock passed. Still nobody came. Kipper pulled off a large piece of cake and broke it open to see if there was a cherry inside. There were two. He ate them both and began to feel better.

By five o'clock there were no more cherries to be found.

Kipper stretched out on the table feeling very full and very sleepy.

Kipper slept through the evening and into the night. He dreamt that he was climbing a mountain made of cake and dodging great cake boulders as they crashed towards him.

Even when the sun streamed through his window the next morning he did not wake, but snored peacefully until noon when he was woken by a knock at the door.

His friends had come.
'Happy birthday,
Kipper!' said Jake.
'Happy birthday,
Kipper!' said Holly.
'And many happy
returns!' said Tiger.
Kipper blinked and
rubbed his eyes.
'But my birthday
was yesterday,' he
said sleepily.

They looked at the invitation.

Plees come to my bithday party tomoro at 12 o cloc dont be lat

Kipper looked puzzled.
'So my birthday is not until tomorrow,' he said. 'We haven't missed it after all!'

'No, no, no,' said Tiger. 'Your birthday must have been *tomorrow* the day before yesterday.' Kipper looked puzzled again.

Tiger went on, 'So yesterday it would have been *today,* but today it was *yesterday.* Do you see?'

Kipper did not see. His brain was beginning to ache so he said, 'Cake anyone?' And then he remembered that he had eaten it all.

'Never mind,' said Tiger. 'Why don't you open your presents?'

The presents seemed a bit odd.
The first was a napkin from Jake.
The second was some candles from Holly.

'Very useful,' said Kipper, trying not to look disappointed.

But the third was the most useful of all…

It was a cake!

Other books by Mick Inkpen

Penguin Small
The Great Pet Sale
The Mick Inkpen Treasury

Everyone Hide from Wibbly Pig
In Wibbly's Garden
Is it Bedtime, Wibbly Pig?
The Wibbly Pig Collection

Kipper's Toybox
Kipper's Book of Counting
Kipper's Book of Colours
Kipper's Book of Opposites
Kipper's Book of Weather
Where, Oh Where, is Kipper's Bear?
Kipper's Snowy Day
Kipper's Christmas Eve
Kipper's A to Z
Kipper and Roly
Kipper's Monster
Kipper's Balloon
Kipper's Beach Ball
The Little Kipper series
Kipper Story Collection
The Little Kipper Collection
The 2nd Little Kipper Collection
Kipper's Box of Books

Blue Nose Island:
Ploo and the Terrible Gnobbler
Beachmoles and Bellvine

British Library Cataloguing in Publication Data

A catalogue record for this book is
available from the British Library

ISBN 1 854 858599 (HB)

Kipper first published 1991
One Bear at Bedtime first published 1987
Billy's Beetle first published 1991
The Blue Balloon first published 1989
Threadbear first published 1993
Lullabyhullaballoo! first published 1993
Nothing first published 1995
Bear first published 1997
Kipper's Birthday first published 1993

This edition first published in 2004
for The Book People Ltd,
Hallwood Avenue, Haydock, St Helens WA11 9UL

Hodder Children's Books,
a division of Hodder Headline Limited
338 Euston Road, London NW1 3BH

10 9 8 7 6 5 4 3 2 1

Printed in China